Stan the Timid Turtle

Helping Children Cope with Fears about School Violence

Laura S. Fox, MA

Illustrated by Anita DuFalla

Dedication

This book is dedicated to all you children who have ever felt like hiding in your bed with the covers over your head. I hope this story gives you the strength to face the day.

Requests for permission should be addressed to:
New Horizon Press
P.O. Box 669
Far Hills, NJ 07931

Laura S. Fox, MA
Stan the Timid Turtle:
    Helping Children Cope with Fears about School Violence

Cover Design and Illustrations: Anita DuFalla
Interior Design: Charley Nasta

Library of Congress Control Number: 2013947758
ISBN 13: 978-0-88282-466-6

SMALL HORIZONS
A Division of New Horizon Press

2018 2017 2016 2015 2014   1 2 3 4 5

Printed in the U.S.A.

It was early morning in Turtlesville. The streets were empty. The town's people were very sad and quiet. Even the trees seemed unable to stand up straight.

Stan, a young turtle, crawled out of his warm, safe bed.

He could hear his parents talking in the kitchen. They were trying to speak softly so he could not hear, but he knew what they were talking about: the news on TV the night before.

A stranger had snuck into a nearby school and hurt a lot of young turtles.

Now Stan felt afraid of everything—most of all his school.

When Stan crept into the kitchen, his mother tried to stop crying and his father hid the newspaper in his robe. They tried to act as if nothing was wrong.

"Good morning, Stan," mother said in a sing-song voice. Stan knew that his parents were trying to keep the bad news from him.

"Do I have to go to school today?" Stan asked.

"Yes," mother answered.

"I think I feel sick." Stan coughed and rubbed his belly.

"You do not feel like you have a fever. I think you are good to go," mother said after touching his forehead.

"NO..." Stan replied.

"What if something bad happens to me?" Stan whispered.

"Nothing bad will happen! You are going to have a great day. You have soccer practice after school and you will have so much fun!" mother said, trying to sound happy.

"How do you know that everything will be okay? You do not know if it will!" Stan yelled. He felt so angry and sad.

"We all need to stay calm and be kind to each other. Worrying will not help anything," father said.

Father stood up from the table. "We need to get on with school and work!"

The family got ready to leave the house.

As Stan walked toward the front door he could feel his heart racing. It was going to beat right out of his chest!

As the door got closer and closer, his knees started to feel weak. He froze.

Then it happened.

Stan hid in his shell and dropped to the floor.

THUMP!

It was nice and dark in his shell. He felt safe.
No one could touch or hurt him.

He decided he would stay inside his shell forever.

Mother and father came running into the room when they heard the thumping noise. They were shocked to see Stan in his shell.

"Oh dear," mother said, looking at father for help.

His father got down on his knees and peered into Stan's shell.

"Knock, knock," he said with a smile and tapped on Stan's shell.

"Not funny! I am sick! I am never, ever coming out! My stomach hurts!" Stan declared and rocked his shell, moving away from his father.

He shut his eyes and tried to think about the summer time when he went swimming at the beach.

Thinking about good things made his heart beat slower.

Stan stayed there for several minutes. His mother and father tried to get him to come out, but he would not leave his shell.

"What if a stranger kidnaps me? What if I come home and you are not here?"

"Stan, you should not worry about things like that," father said.

"You are a young turtle who should have fun and not be afraid," mother said.

"I guess we should call Dr. Hope. She will know what to do," mother decided and she phoned the doctor right away.

Dr. Hope was a very good doctor. Stan wanted to be a doctor just like her one day. She always made him feel better.

"Dr. Hope will not be able to change my mind!" Stan yelled from inside his shell.

Stan stayed in his shell as his father carried him out to the car.

He stayed in his shell for the entire car ride to Dr. Hope's office.

He stayed in his shell even when his father put him on the examination table.

"Oh my!" Dr. Hope said, walking into the room.

She put her face right up against the opening of Stan's shell, pretending to examine it. Shaking her head, she said, "Well, Stan, your shell looks fine to me."

Stan opened his eyes to see her kind smile. Just seeing Dr. Hope made him feel better.

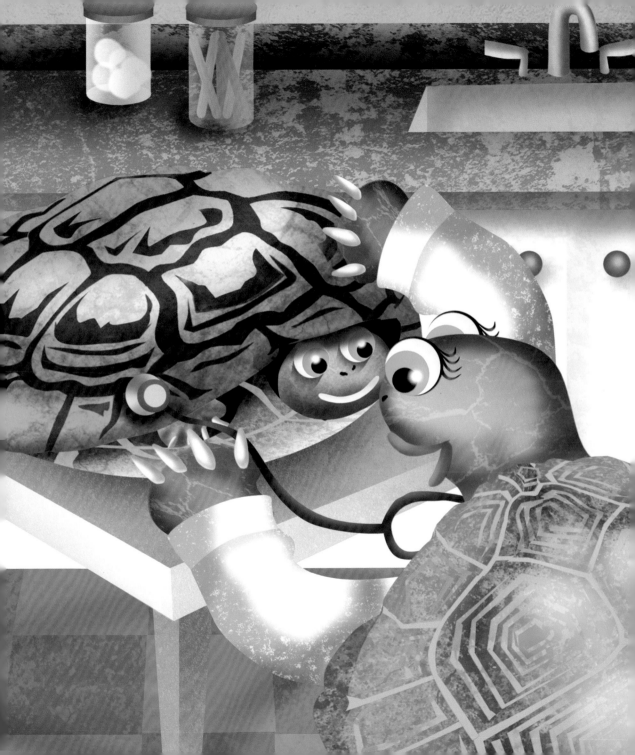

"Stan, I know you are scared," she said.
"I have a secret to tell you. I am a little scared too."

"You are scared too?" Stan was surprised.

"Yes. When that school was attacked and little turtles were hurt, that was very frightening. However, scary things do happen. It is okay to be afraid when you hear about bad things happening."

"Is it?" Stan asked.

"Yes, as long as you do not let fear get in the way of doing what you should, like learning and having fun," Dr. Hope said.

"Like going to school?" Stan asked guiltily.

"Yes," Dr. Hope nodded. "Your school will have new alarms and even some guards. Everyone wants this town to be safer, especially for the little turtles. You need to come out of your shell and help us," Dr. Hope said.

"Me? What can I do? I am just a little turtle!"

"We need you to help by telling us when you see or hear something strange, when other young turtles seem like they are going to do something bad or are in trouble. These are times when you need to tell the teachers and the guards. We need you to watch out for the younger turtles, too," Dr. Hope explained.

"Yes, like your cousin Lilly, who follows you around. She is probably more scared than you, Stan," Mother added.

Stan remembered that in the summer at the beach, Lilly would not go into the water until Stan checked it out first.

This made him realize he had to come out of his shell.

"Sometimes, when I feel scared, I repeat some special words to myself to calm down," Dr. Hope explained.

"Be brave. Be true. Do not let fear overcome you. Stay strong and carry on."

Stan liked the words. They gave him hope. He took a deep breath and shut his eyes. He pictured himself being brave so Lilly and other little turtles would not be afraid.

With one big stretch, he pulled himself out of his shell and opened his eyes.

Be bRave. Be TRue.
Do NOT LeT feaR
OveRCOMe YOU.

STaY STRONG
aND CaRRY ON.

Stan repeated, "Be brave. Be true. Do not let fear overcome you. Stay strong and carry on."

Stan started to feel better.

"I have a poster for you to put up in your room. On it are the words I just taught you. Practice saying them to yourself every night before you go to bed, so when you feel scared you will remember them. Will you do that for me?" Dr. Hope asked.

Stan nodded yes with his eyes wide open.

"Thank you, Dr. Hope."

Later that week, Stan was walking to the boy turtles' bathroom when he noticed two strangers, a man and a woman.

He had never seen these two people before.

He felt fear grip him. The urge to hide in his shell was powerful. Stan shut his eyes and repeated Dr. Hope's words to himself: "Be brave. Be true. Do not let fear overcome you. Stay strong and carry on."

Stan knew what he had to do. Stan walked over to Officer Shelly, who was coming down the hallway.

"What is wrong?" asked Officer Shelly.

"There are strangers in the school," Stan said in a clear, strong voice. "I do not think they should be here and I do not want anybody to be hurt."

Stan showed Officer Shelly where he had seen the man and woman. Officer Shelly then spoke to the principal, who called the police.

"You were right, Stan. They are not supposed to be here," Officer Shelly said.

Stan waited for the fear to come, but no butterflies invaded his belly and no tears came from his eyes. He looked at Officer Shelly and felt proud.

That night, with mother and father, Stan watched the news on TV and saw a report about how Stan had told the guard about the strangers in his school.

All the little turtles had hidden in safe places and then left before anybody got hurt.

"We are so proud of you," mother smiled.

Father nodded. "You were scared, but you got help so you and everyone else could be safe! Dr. Hope will be proud of you too."

A week later, when Stan's school reopened, the principal announced, "There will be a special program in the auditorium."

The principal and Officer Shelly presented Stan with a blue ribbon and a sash. The sash said "Hall Monitor." Everyone agreed that Stan would be the perfect hall monitor to protect the school from danger!

"Thank you," Stan smiled. "I learned that it is okay to feel like hiding in your shell, but you cannot let your fear keep you from going to school and having fun. Please remember this saying:

'Be brave. Be true. Do not let fear overcome you. Stay strong and carry on.'"

All the turtles cheered.

Stan became the best hall monitor
the Turtlesville School ever had.

THE END

Tips for Children

1. Breathe deeply, watching your belly move up and down. As you exhale, imagine all your worries being blown away. This will help to calm you. You will notice your shoulders relaxing.

2. Imagine a warm blanket around yourself, giving you comfort.

3. If you have a special toy that makes you feel safe, hold it when you are feeling frightened. I have a Raggedy Ann doll that my Grandma gave me. When no one is around and I am feeling sad or upset, sometimes I still hold her!

4. Tell yourself that you are safe. Tell yourself that you are strong and not going to let any harm come to yourself.

5. Think about happy things like Stan did.

6. Have a plan if the thing you are afraid of should happen. For example, find out where the exits are and how to call 911.

7. Do not keep your fears to yourself. Talk with a counselor, teacher, caregiver, or parent.

8. All of us need to work together to make this world safer. One thing that we all can do is keep our eyes and ears aware of anything suspicious. If you think someone may be going to do something bad, tell an adult immediately.

9. Remind yourself that everyone feels afraid at some time, even grown ups. Take positive action so that you begin to feel better and better, stronger and stronger.

10. If you are thinking about a bad event that happened, imagine locking it in a box and throwing away the key.

Tips for Parents, Caregivers and Educators

1. If you are an adult and your children are afraid, talk it out. Let them give you the information and do not overload them with scary facts. If the fear begins to interfere with their lives, seek the advice of a counselor.

2. With so many distractions it can be hard to give children our full attention. Be sure to take the time to talk to them and show them you are listening by looking directly at them. Sometimes just telling another person our fears helps. Be sure not to dismiss children's feelings but rather acknowledge their concerns.

3. If you are an adult who suffers from anxiety, try not to talk with your children about your own fears. Role model for your children positive ways of dealing with anxiety, like taking deep breaths.

4. Remind your children of all the times that they experienced what they were afraid of and nothing bad happened, all the times that they went to school and they were safe. No harm came to them.

5. Ask your children what could they say to themselves when they are feeling scared. Most likely they will say, "I am brave."

6. If something bad does happen, it is better that your children hear about it from you. Explain the situation in a calm way and let them ask questions. Don't overwhelm them with details. Reassure them about their own safety and discuss ways they can help.

7. Limit your children's access to television news reports after a tragic event. Viewing such events over and over may trigger added anxiety for both children and adults. Emphasize stories of survival and calmly review the safety rules.

8. Compartmentalize the discussion. Don't dwell on it; suggest that it is time to do something that affirms normality.

9. The skills you are teaching your children regarding anxiety will help them face situations head on and problem solve throughout their lives.